A FRIEND FOR CHRISTMAS

A FRIEND FOR
CHRISTMAS

Lauren St John

Illustrated by Matt Robertson

Orion
Children's Books

ORION CHILDREN'S BOOKS

First published in Great Britain in 2016
by Hodder and Stoughton

1 3 5 7 9 10 8 6 4 2

Text © Lauren St John, 2016
Illustrations © Matt Robertson, 2016

The moral rights of the author and illustrator have been asserted.

A CIP catalogue record for this book
is available from the British Library.

ISBN 978 1 4440 0806 7

Printed and bound in China

The paper and board used in this book are from well-managed forests
and other responsible sources.

MIX
Paper from
responsible sources
FSC
www.fsc.org **FSC® C104740**

Orion Children's Books
An imprint of
Hachette Children's Group
Part of Hodder and Stoughton
Carmelite House
50 Victoria Embankment
London EC4Y 0DZ

An Hachette UK Company
www.hachette.co.uk

www.hachettechildrens.co.uk

For Hugo and Dulcie.

Contents

Chapter 1

"If you could have anything in the world for Christmas, what would it be?" asked Luka's dad.

He was a tall man who always looked as if he'd been caught in a cyclone, even when all he'd done was type numbers into his computer.

"How about a skateboard,

a surfboard

or a pair of trainers?"

Luka shook his head.
"No, thanks."

His mum was putting sparkly stars on the tree.

"Tell us your number one wish. Would you like a new football, a book, or a computer game?"

"No, thank you," said Luka. He didn't believe in wishes. What was the point? For a hundred days, he'd wished until he was dizzy, but his red and grey mongrel hadn't come home.

Life wasn't the same without
Buddy.

His mum and dad had tried hard to
make up for it. They'd bought him
a red bike with lots of gears.

For his birthday, they'd given him a chemistry set.

It had six purple bottles that went
fizz, crackle and pop.

But none of these gifts made Luka smile because they weren't Buddy. The mongrel he had rescued from the animal shelter was the thing he wished for most of all.

"If I can't have my best friend, I don't want anything," he said.

His mum sighed. "Luka, it's a hundred days since Buddy went missing. I'm sure somebody found him and gave him a loving home. He's probably forgotten about us."

That night, Luka couldn't sleep.
He stared out of the window at a
yellow moon shaped like a banana.

He wondered if Buddy could see it too. He didn't believe that Buddy had forgotten him.

If he could remember Buddy, surely Buddy could remember him?

Chapter 2

A thousand miles away, a red and grey mongrel with one floppy ear lay gazing at a yellow moon shaped like a banana.

For a hundred days he'd pined for
a boy with sticking-up brown hair –
a boy called Luka who loved him.

But Buddy was lost and didn't
know the way home.

His adventures began when he chased after Luka's school bus. It sped away and left him in the dust.

Two boys were playing frisbee on the beach. Buddy tried to join in but they chased him away.

A little girl gave him an ice cream.

While he was eating it, he spotted a
shark stalking a surfer.

He swam into the sea and barked.
The shark swished its tail crossly
but it went away to eat fish.

The grateful surfer took Buddy for
a ride on a wave.

They went to the Sydney Opera
House, where the surfer had a
job. Buddy was so bored that he
wandered onto the stage.

There were lots of bright lights.
When the curtain went up, Buddy
did tricks and people cheered.

"Hire that dog! He's a star!" cried
the director.

But Buddy missed Luka. He ran
away to find him in the city.

He ended up on a carnival float,
sitting in the mouth of a dragon…

A hairy biker rescued him and took
him to a music festival.

It was fun but too loud.
Buddy went looking for some
peace and quiet…

He was found by a sailor, who took him to the Great Barrier Reef. Buddy ate lobsters on a yacht.

He even met cockatoos
in the rainforest.

When the sailor sailed away,
Buddy went walkabout in the
Outback.

It was so hot that Buddy jumped
into a pool to get cool and was
nearly eaten by a crocodile.

A tourist saved him and took him up Ayers Rock. When he came down, Buddy chased a kangaroo. It gave him a boxing lesson.

He hitched a ride on a truck. It took him to a farm, where a cattle dog said that Luka had probably forgotten him.

Buddy didn't believe her. If he could remember Luka, surely Luka could remember him?

Chapter 3

That night, Buddy was so sad that
he climbed into the deepest basket
he could find and went to sleep.

When he woke up he thought the basket was on fire. A man climbed in. Buddy was in a balloon, heading for the moon.

He was as surprised to meet Father
Christmas as Father Christmas
was to meet him. "Where are your
reindeer?" Buddy asked.

"They eat too much," said Father Christmas. "The last lot kept stopping for mince pies.

Balloons are quicker. I suppose you're hoping for a Christmas present? What's your greatest wish?

A juicy bone?

A new ball?

A smart kennel?"

Buddy shook his head. "All I want is my best friend. I want to go home to Luka but I don't know how to find him."

"We'll see about that," said Father
Christmas.

Chapter 4

On Christmas morning, Luka rushed to see if Buddy was under the tree.

There were lots of presents,
but none were shaped like a
mongrel with one floppy ear.
His heart sank.

His mum and dad were miserable too. They stared at the gifts nobody wanted.

There was a big crash. Soot rained down the chimney. A dog landed in the fireplace. He was the same size as Buddy but he was pitch black.

"What a shame," said Luka's mum.
"For a moment I thought it was
Buddy."

"It is Buddy!" cried Luka.
The little mongrel barked with joy.
He bounded up to Luka and licked
his face.

Then he raced in so many circles
of happiness that the soot flew off
and they could see his red and grey
coat.

The tree had fallen over and the presents were in tatters. Nobody minded because Buddy and Luka were together again. And friendship, as everyone knows, is the best gift of all.